THE MEADOW

Story by ELIEL LUMA FIONN

Pictures by NANCY BRIGHT

Library of Congress Control Number: 2013908208

ISBN 978-0-9893054-0-2

Summary: When a magical storyteller visits a little kingdom, the inhabitants lives are
changed forever.

Printed in China

For Maia Rianne Hisamoto,

who approved this book,

and for all of those preschool kids over the years

who said, "Write it down."

Once long ago there was a little kingdom where everyone worked hard and lived happily together in peace.

One day an old, old man, so ancient that his beard was white as soft clouds on a spring day, came to the little kingdom. He moved slowly through the village streets, and the people were very kind to him. They brought him fresh water to drink, a loaf of bread to eat, and inquired politely where he was headed. The old man smiled and said, "I've come to find a place where the animals graze freely and the birds sing sweetly."

Hearing this, one of the youngest children took him by the hand and offered to show him the Meadow. The old man and the little boy walked out of the town and down the road to the most beautiful meadow, where horses and cows, sheep and pigs roamed freely. All manner of birds built their homes in nearby trees, while wildflowers carpeted the ground in colorful abundance.

The old man laughed in delight, and settling himself down on a grassy hillock, he closed his eyes.

"But what will you do here?" asked the child in bewilderment, for it seemed to him a strange sort of place to take a nap.

"I will listen to the plants and animals tell their stories," said the old man quietly. "Listen! Can you hear the birds singing tales of dangerous journeys and wondrous sights?"

The little boy lay down next to the old man, closed his eyes, and listened closely. "I can hear the wind in the trees," said the child, "and the sound of the bees, and the song of the birds in their nests, but I don't hear any stories. Would you tell me a story?"

The old man described his adventures across the world, the people and places he'd seen, and the magical creatures he'd met. It was all so interesting and wise and surprising that the little boy didn't want him to stop. At last the old man finished.

"Child," he said, "you must run along home now before your people begin to worry."

The child thanked the old man very politely, and then asked if he could please come back and hear another story. The old man agreed, for he loved telling stories and never ran out of things to say.

The following day the child returned with three of his friends and found the old man still sitting on the same grassy knoll. They all sat enthralled at the old man's tales of faraway places and strange beasts they'd never seen. At last it grew very late and the old man sent them home, but not before the child noticed that the old man's beard looked much longer than it had the day before.

The next day the child returned with more of his friends to hear the old man's stories. At the end of the day the old man's beard had again grown noticeably longer. Each day after that the child brought even more friends, and soon the old man's beard was so long and thick they made themselves a nest in it to listen comfortably. At last nearly all of the children in the village were spending hours sitting at the old man's feet, rapt in his stories.

A few of the mothers, who had been bringing the old man food since he had been occupying their children so nicely, stopped to listen as well. They became as engrossed as their children, often forgetting their chores.

"Goodness," they cried, "we're late with supper, we must get home."

The very next day they were back, and soon their husbands, looking for their dinners, wound up listening as well. They brought their friends and families from other villages, and by then the old man's beard had grown wide enough to cover a large portion of the meadow so there was plenty of room for everyone.

The horses and cows, sheep and pigs took naps in the old man's beard. The birds paused in their songs to listen, and even the bees forgot to buzz. Some days the only sound in the Meadow was the old man telling his stories to the wonderment of the crowd.

Finally, after a few weeks, the king noticed that many of his courtiers kept disappearing, as did his meals and comforts. He followed the throng of people to the Meadow one morning and interrupted the storyteller after only the first tale.

"Excuse me, Old One," said his majesty. "You tell the most marvelous stories that I've ever heard, and your beard is soft as downy feathers. But my people are neglecting their usual duties, and I cannot run the kingdom by myself. Please, leave off your storytelling and let them return to their lives. You confuse our young folk with your talk of travel and faraway sights. Let them be content with what they have."

The old man stood up slowly and bowed to the king. "As you wish, Sir," he replied. "I will leave here as you have asked, but there are those who may wish to accompany me. It is easy to be content with what one has when it is all one knows, but there are many choices and marvels in life. Let those who would find their own way in the world decide for themselves."

The old man looked out at the crowd as the people began to rise and go home, heeding their king's words. There were a few couples, however, who remained seated, excited to know that they could journey afar. And one child, the very first who had listened to the old man's stories, sat joyfully and calmly in the center of the Meadow. He kept resisting his mother's attempts to pull him away, and no matter how she tried, it seemed he was stuck to the old man's beard. At last his mother let him be, as one of the couples assured her they would look after him, and send her word during their travels. She hugged her little boy goodbye and left to follow the others.

As the townspeople turned for a final farewell to the old man and their kinfolk, they saw a strange sight. The old man's beard, with the people still sitting inside, began to rise up until the edges closed together and formed a balloon.

The old man, waving gaily, shouted, "Up we go!" and the huge beard balloon floated up high into the sky with the old man dangling beneath it. At last it was just a tiny speck.

Years and many adventures later, when the traveling child had grown to be a man, he returned to the little kingdom. It was still peaceful, and when he walked down the village streets people were very kind to him, giving him a flask of water and a loaf of bread to eat. When they asked him where he was going he said, "a place to sit where the animals graze freely and the birds sing sweetly."

A little boy offered to show him the way, and taking the young boy's hand, the man, who loved to tell stories, followed him out of the village and into the Meadow.

The Meadow

There's a place where I go

that the animals know,

a meadow that's deep green and wide,

the earth sings a song

and the birds chirp along

and all kinds of creatures abide.

The cows, pigs, and sheep

have no schedule to keep,

the bugs sit still and attend,

they all listen to stories

of the teller who glories

in travels of mind without end.

To visit this place

takes silence and grace

and the kind of courage of heart,

that exists in a child

who doesn't mind wild

adventures of life from the start.

About the Author

Eliel Fionn has been writing stories and poetry since the age of eight. She has published two fiction novels, *Rebecca Bloom*, and *Return From Purple Earth*, a book of poetry, *Somewhere an Opening*, and a quarterly newsletter, *Feltie World News*. An artist, writer, and intuitive, Eliel and her husband Mark live in Eugene, Oregon.

Please visit her website at www.elielfionn.com.

About the Illustrator

Nancy Bright has been creating art in various forms since early childhood. A self-taught watercolor artist, she is recognized world wide for her deeply moving spiritual imagery. She lives in Eugene, Oregon with her son and one fat cat, and spends many reflective hours creating her backyard garden sanctuary.

To view more of Nancy's exquisite artwork, please visit her website at www.brightcreationsart.com.